JENNIFER, TOO

JENNIFER, TOO

Juanita Havill

illustrated by
J. J. Smith-Moore

Hyperion Books for Children

New York

For my big brother Frank, who will always
be Wall to me

—J. H.

To Mom and Fah, who made it all possible
for this Jennifer

—J. J. S. M.

Text © 1994 by Juanita Havill.
Illustrations © 1994 by J. J. Smith-Moore.

Jacket illustration ©1995 by Jennifer Plecas.

Printed in the United States of America.

FIRST EDITION
1 3 5 7 9 10 8 6 4 2

The artwork for each picture is prepared using
pen and ink and ink wash.
This book is set in 16-point Palatino.

Library of Congress Cataloging-in-Publication Data
Havill, Juanita.
Jennifer, too / Juanita Havill; illustrated by J. J. Smith-Moore.—1st ed.
p.   cm.
Summary: Jennifer discovers ways to be included in the games
of her older brother, Matt, and his friends.
ISBN 1-56282-618-2 (trade)—ISBN 1-56282-619-0 (lib. bdg.)
ISBN 0-7868-1072-6 (pbk.)
[1. Play—Fiction. 2. Brothers and sisters—Fiction.] I. Smith-Moore,
J. J., ill. II. Title.
PZ7.H3115Je   1994
[Fic]—dc20   93-6319

Contents

1.   Spies in Disguise

"Hey, Matt!" Jennifer ran up to her big brother Matt. He was in the backyard with his friend T. J. "Where were you? I've been looking all over for you. I looked in the backyard before, but you weren't there."

"I was at T. J.'s house," said Matt.

"Can I play with you and T. J.?"

Jennifer asked.

"No," said Matt. "I didn't bring T. J. here to play with you. Go bother someone else."

"There's nobody else to bother," Jennifer said. "There's never anybody else. Not in the whole neighborhood. Just you and and your friends."

If only some kids her age lived in the neighborhood, Jennifer would have someone to play with. She would be especially happy if a seven-year-old girl would move into the neighborhood. She had lived here all her life, and still there were no girls. Everybody had boys—big ones, too, like her brother Matt.

"Look, we're busy," said Matt.

"Go away," said T. J.

Big, unfriendly boys, Jennifer thought. She didn't have anything to do right now. She didn't want to go away. If they wouldn't let her play, she would just keep talking to them. "Why are you wearing raincoats?" she asked. "It's sunny."

Matt put his finger to his lips. "We're spies, Jennifer. Don't blab it."

"In disguise," T. J. whispered.

"What's a disguise?" said Jennifer.

"It's something you wear so people won't recognize you," Matt said.

"What do you mean 'recognize'?"

T. J. threw up his hands, but Matt explained. "You wear a disguise when you don't want people to know who you are."

"Then *you* aren't in disguise," Jennifer said. "Because I know who you are."

"You don't count," said T. J.

"I do, too. I can count to a thousand, easy. One, two, three, four—"

"That's not what I mean." Matt's whisper got louder and louder. "You don't count because we're not spying on you. So it doesn't matter if *you* recognize us."

"Oh," said Jennifer. "If you're not spying on me, could I be a spy with you?"

Matt shook his head. T. J. frowned.

"Why not?"

"Being spies is too dangerous," Matt said.

"But you are spies."

"We're older," said Matt, "and we're boys."

"You always say that when you don't want me to play," Jennifer said. She thought about how Matt and his friends got to play in a baseball tournament at the park. And when they built a tree-house, Dad let them use his plywood and hammer and nails. They always hogged the video games at the mall, too. Jennifer didn't get to do any of these things, but they could because they were boys and they were older.

"Come on, Matt," T. J. said. "We're wasting time. Let's go."

"All right, T. J." Matt and T. J. turned away from Jennifer and began to talk in low voices about their plan. "Remember the territory you're covering. Your orders are to find out as much as you can on your mission. But whatever you do, don't get caught. If you do get caught, don't talk. Got it?"

"Right," said T. J.

"Meet me in ten minutes. You know where." Matt turned to Jennifer. "And Jennifer, don't follow us."

"Yeah," said T. J. in a warning tone, and they took off.

Jennifer watched Matt run up the sidewalk and around the corner. T. J. cut across the backyard to the alley. Jennifer didn't follow. How could she follow them both? They were going in different directions.

Jennifer had a better idea. She went to the laundry room in her house. The laundry room was next to the kitchen. Matt and his friends always came to the kitchen for a snack and then had secret meetings in the laundry room. That's where they would come in ten minutes.

Jennifer looked for a place to hide. The big yellow clothes basket was full of clean clothes that needed to be sorted. Not now, thought Jennifer. I have important work to do—spy work. She jerked a sheet out to make room. She scrunched down in the sheets in the basket. Then she waited for the boys to arrive.

She waited and waited. She moved around to get more comfortable. Then

she wiggled her ankles to keep her feet from going to sleep. Ten minutes is a really long time, she thought. Or maybe it has been more than ten minutes. What if something had happened to them? Matt said that being spies is dangerous. Maybe someone had caught them. She should find out.

Jennifer stood up. She started to climb out of the basket, but when she heard voices, she dropped back down in the sheets. She pulled a pillowcase over her head to make sure no one recognized her.

Matt and T. J. rushed into the laundry room. Matt closed the door. "We'll make a tent," he said, "with a sheet."

Jennifer peeked through a tear in the

pillowcase. She could see Matt coming toward the basket. Oh no! He was going to take the sheet she was hiding in. She held her breath.

Matt reached toward the basket. Jennifer closed her eyes. She knew what would happen next. Matt would find

her and he would be mad. She waited for him to shout, "Jennifer, go away. Don't bother us ever again!"

But Matt didn't shout anything. Jennifer opened her eyes. Whew! She let out her breath. Matt had picked up the sheet from the floor. He threw it over the ironing board, and he and T. J. crawled into their tent.

Jennifer strained to hear what they were saying.

"What did you find out, Agent 06?" Matt asked.

"I covered the whole corner like you told me. I saw the garbage truck. And Mrs. Clancy's cat."

"Is that all?" scoffed Matt. "Well, listen to this. Remember how we thought we saw Mrs. Babbitt put a bomb in the garbage? It wasn't a bomb. It was a broken lamp. Also, a strange blue car is parked in the Colberts' driveway— license number SOS-333. And I heard voices coming from Mr. Weaver's house. But Mr. Weaver is on vacation.

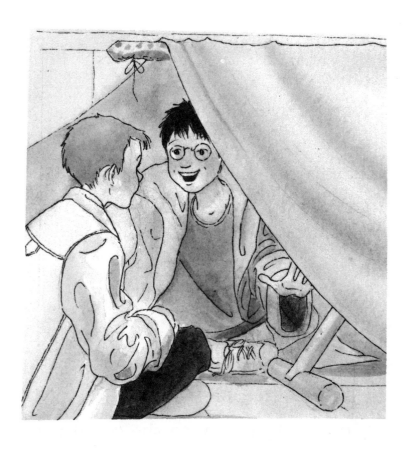

There's not supposed to be anyone there."

"Robbers?" asked T. J.

"We should go back and investigate."

"Do we have to?"

"Good spies always find out as much as they can," said Matt.

Jennifer waited until the boys were out of sight. Then she slipped the pillowcase off and jumped up to follow them. She took the pillowcase with her all the way to Mr. Weaver's. She might need to use it as a disguise.

Matt and T. J. were hiding under bushes beside the driveway. Jennifer put the pillowcase over her head. It draped around her shoulders and she found the torn spot so she could peek out. She crouched down and sneaked toward them.

It was hard to walk because she couldn't see the ground very well. "Oof!" She tripped on a rock and fell

15

flat on her stomach.

"Who's there?" Matt said.

"I bet it's a robber," T. J. said. "A short robber."

Jennifer pulled the pillowcase off. "I am not a robber!"

"It's Jennifer," T. J. said with disgust.

"Why are you wearing a pillow-case?" Matt asked.

"It's my disguise. I'm a spy."

"Spies don't wear pillowcases, Jennifer."

"I do. And I'm a good spy. I found out lots."

"Like what?" said T. J.

Jennifer thought about what she had heard the boys say in the laundry room. "I found out that Mrs. Babbitt put a broken lamp in the garbage. I found out that there's a blue car in the Colberts' driveway. The license plate number is SOS-333. And there are voices at Mr. Weaver's house."

"How did she find that out?" T. J. whispered.

Matt shrugged. "Who cares? We already knew that, Jennifer."

"I didn't," said Jennifer. "I discovered it. See, I'm a good spy. Now I want to know

about the voices at Mr. Weaver's, too."

"That's what we're trying to do," said Matt.

"But you interrupted us," T. J. added.

"Can I spy with you?"

"I guess," said Matt. "But keep behind us, and try not to trip."

Jennifer put the pillowcase back over her head. She would be very careful. She wanted to show Matt and T. J. that she could be a good spy.

She and Matt and T. J. crept closer to the house. They waited behind the bushes and watched.

"Look," Matt said. "Someone's coming."

Jennifer couldn't see very well so she pulled the pillowcase off. She watched a woman walk past Mr. Weaver's back door and go down the driveway. The woman held a key in her hand and headed toward the front door.

"What's she doing?" T. J. asked.

"I don't know," Matt said, "but she'd better be careful."

Jennifer jumped up.

"Jennifer, get down. You'll blow our cover," hissed T. J.

"Jennifer, that's not the way to play spies." Matt sounded mad.

But Jennifer didn't stop. She ran right up to the woman on Mr. Weaver's front steps.

"Stop!" she shouted. "There are robbers in there."

"Robbers?" The woman listened at the front door.

Jennifer did, too. She could hear a

man's voice. Then she heard music.

"Those aren't robbers." The woman shook her head. "It's the radio."

"Did the robbers turn the radio on?"

"No," said the woman. "Mr. Weaver turned it on. He forgot to turn it off, too. He often does."

"But Mr. Weaver isn't home."

"I know. I'm his sister. I came to take care of his house. I just got the key he left with the neighbors." She put the key in the door. "Are you watching the house for Mr. Weaver?"

"Sort of," said Jennifer. "We are spies in disguise."

"We?" said the woman. "Where are the other spies?"

Jennifer pointed to the bushes, but Matt and T. J. were gone. They aren't very good spies, she thought.

"Thanks for watching the house," the woman said. She opened the door to go inside.

"You're welcome."

Jennifer walked home slowly. She was thinking about all of the things she had found out from Mr. Weaver's sister. When she got home, she sat on the front step to think some more. Maybe she would tell Matt and T. J. But maybe she wouldn't. Ater all, they hadn't even stayed around.

Jennifer heard a car horn honk and she looked up. Mr. Weaver's sister was driving by in a blue car. She waved at

Jennifer. Jennifer jumped up and waved back. When the car passed, she saw the license plate. "SOS-333," she read out loud. "Oh, wow!" This was something she had to tell Matt and T. J.

She found them in the laundry room.

"Matt, guess what!"

Matt poked his head out of the tent.

"There aren't any robbers, Matt. It's Mr. Weaver's radio. He left it on, and his sister came to turn it off. She came in a blue car, and do you know what the license number is? SOS-333."

"So what?" said Matt.

"So I'm a good spy. I found out lots. Let's play some more. It's fun."

"Jennifer, you're not a good spy. You blew our cover. You talk too much."

"Yeah, and you have a silly disguise," T. J. said from inside the tent.

"Don't bother us," Matt said, and ducked back into the tent.

Jennifer stomped out of the laundry room. "I'm a better spy than you are. You just don't want me to play."

She plopped down by the door to wait. If Matt and T. J. went spying again, she was going with them.

2. Ghosts in the Attic

Jennifer sat in front of the laundry-room door, waiting. When are Matt and T. J. ever going to come out? she wondered.

"Jennifer, is Matt home?" Matt's friend David stood at the screen door.

Jennifer pointed to the closed door. "He's in there. Come in."

28

"He must be having a meeting," David said. He opened the door and walked through the kitchen. "What are you doing here, Jennifer?"

"I'm playing spies in disguise." Jennifer got up.

"Spies in disguise is boring," said David.

"It's not boring to me."

David went into the laundry room, and Jennifer followed.

"Hey, Matt! Hey, T. J.!" David called. "What's up?"

T. J. crawled out of the tent. "We're playing spies, but I'm tired of it."

Matt crawled out after T. J. "Me, too," he said.

"I'm not," Jennifer said.

"So let's play something else," Matt said.

"I've got an idea," said David. "Do you want to play ghosts in the attic?"

"Sure," said Matt. "We can go up to our attic."

"That'll be fun," said T. J.

"Why can't we play spies in disguise?" Jennifer said.

"Sorry, Jennifer. We can't," Matt said. "You're outnumbered. Three to one. We want to play ghosts in the attic."

"Do we have to go up to the attic?" Jennifer had been in the attic before. She didn't like the strange smell. It tickled her nose. And all the thick dust made her cough. It was too dark and dingy in the attic.

"We have to. Attics are spooky places," said David. "You always tell ghost stories in spooky places."

"Yeah," said Matt. "You either go to the cemetery at midnight, and we can't do that because Mom won't let us. Or you go down in a damp, dark cellar, except we don't have one. So we're going to the attic, where it's pitch black."

"Couldn't we turn the light on?" Jennifer said.

"No way," said Matt.

"We told you. It has to be dark. You can't tell ghost stories with the light on," said David.

"I don't see why not," Jennifer said. "We could take a flashlight. You'll need

a flashlight to read the stories."

"But we're not reading stories," Matt said. "We're *telling* stories—true ghost stories."

"True ghost stories?" Jennifer said.

"Yeah. About real live ghosts," said David.

"Teeerrible. Scaaarrry. Haaaaaaunting ghosts." T. J. sounded weird. Then he said, "Let's go."

"Wait," said Jennifer. "I don't like scary stories in the dark. They give me nightmares."

"Jennifer, that's how you play. If you don't want to play ghosts in the attic, then don't come," Matt said.

"But I want to," said Jennifer. "If you'll just leave the light on."

The boys all shook their heads. Jennifer knew they wouldn't change their minds. "You're just doing that so I won't come," she said.

"Suit yourself." Matt shrugged. He and David and T. J. went upstairs. They opened a door at the end of the hall and went up the creaky steps to another door—the door to the attic.

Jennifer followed them upstairs, but she didn't go all the way to the attic. She didn't like it to be dark up there. When she was in the attic, she always turned the light on so she wouldn't bump into boxes and trunks. She never went there without Matt and he didn't mind the light then. But today he wanted to play with his friends, not her. That's why he wouldn't turn the light on.

Jennifer went to her room and sat on the bed. She could hear their voices in the attic. She thought she heard the boys say her name. Then they laughed. Ghost stories aren't supposed to be funny. Jennifer wondered if they were really telling ghost stories, or were they laughing at her?

She jumped up and got her flashlight. She woke up her cat, who was asleep on the bed.

"Come on, Guinevere."

Jennifer went to the hall door. She opened it and sat down on the steps. So did Guinevere.

Jennifer had to strain to hear what David was saying.

"In a dark, dark woods . . ."

What kind of a scary story was that? David made his voice spooky. He laughed a ghoulish laugh.

Jennifer wanted to find out what was so scary. She listened to the whole story. That's not scary, she thought. It's only a story about a little ghost in a house.

"Now it's my turn," T. J. said. He told

36

a story about rotting bones in a deep, dank grave. On Friday the thirteenth at midnight a gravedigger undug the bones and up they jumped and danced a jig and chased the man away.

That's not so scary either, Jennifer thought. It's silly.

It was Matt's turn. "Now I will tell you about the ghost of Gone," he said. Then he whispered very low.

Jennifer couldn't hear. She stood up. She beamed the flashlight on the attic steps and started going up. Guinevere followed.

Creak, creak went the steps.

"What's that?" said T. J.

Jennifer stopped.

"Your imagination," said Matt. "The

cemetery was dark and quiet," he continued.

Creak, creak. Jennifer and Guinevere took another step.

"Didn't you hear that?" said David.

"*I* did," said T. J. "There's something out there."

"It's only the wind," said Matt. He

went on with his story. "The wind blew through the trees and made a moaning sound. Be-ware. Be-ware. Be-ware the ghost of Gone."

Creak! Creak! Creak!

Jennifer reached the top of the stairs. She opened the door a crack. Guinevere ran between her legs and she accidentally stepped on Guinevere's paw.

"Meow-ow-ow!" Guinevere howled, and ran into the attic.

"Yikes!" shouted David. He scrambled toward the door. He shoved it wide open and ran out. The door bumped Jennifer and scrunched her against the wall. She heard someone else run out. Then she crept from behind the door. She beamed her flash-

light around the attic. The spotlight landed on Matt. He was getting up from the floor.

"Those stories weren't very scary," said Jennifer.

Matt turned on the attic light. "My story is, too, scary. You interrupted me. What are you doing here anyway?" Matt asked. "You said you weren't going to come."

"I want to tell a scary story, too," said Jennifer.

"But I thought you didn't like scary stories. They give you nightmares. Do you want to have horrible nightmares?"

"I'm not scared now," said Jennifer. "Not with you here and Guinevere and

the light turned on. I think David and T. J. are scared. They ran away. You're not scared, are you Matt?"

"Scared? Me? Of course, not," said Matt. "If you want to tell a story, go ahead."

Jennifer stayed in the attic and told Matt the scariest story she knew. She had heard it on the car radio at Halloween when Mom took them trick-or-treating. It was about a three-legged ghost that ran around at night.

"*Klop, klop, klop. Klop, klop, klop,*" she said. "Better not go out when the moon is down. Ooo-ooo-ooo! I'll grab you and hold you and never let you go. Ooo-ooo-ooo!"

They left the light on.

3. Knights in Armor

After lunch Matt's friends came back. They were ready to play something else. No one mentioned ghosts in the attic.

Matt's friend Kenneth came running up. "Hey, guys! What are you doing?" he said.

"Nothing yet," Matt said.

"Let's play knights in armor," Kenneth said.

"Knights in armor is my favorite," Jennifer said. "I want to play knights in armor, too." Jennifer had read stories about knights in Matt's books. She loved to look at the pictures. Knights wore shiny armor and helmets and carried swords and shields and long pointed lances. They rode horses and looked for dangerous dragons in the countryside. Sometimes they rescued princesses and went on quests for golden goblets. Jennifer wanted to be a knight.

"What do you guys think?" Matt asked. "Do you want to play knights?"

"Yeah," Jennifer and the boys said.

45

"Okay. You have to have a shield to be a knight," Matt said. "Guys, go get your garbage can lids, and you can all be knights."

The boys ran home. Jennifer ran to look for a shield, but Matt got there first. When the boys came back, they all had round, silver shields. Jennifer didn't have one.

"I will be King Matt the Lionhearted," said Matt. He held up a stick for a sword. "I dub you Sir David. And you, Sir T. J. And you, Sir Kenneth."

"Hooray!" The knights held up their shields and swords.

"Hey, what about me? I want to play, too," said Jennifer.

Matt lowered his shield and looked

at Jennifer.

He was thinking. Jennifer knew that was not a good sign. He would come up with an idea she wouldn't like.

Finally Matt said, "Then you can be queen."

Jennifer was afraid of that. "I don't want to be queen," said Jennifer.

"Guinevere can be queen."

"Guinevere can't be queen," said Matt. "She's a cat."

"Yeah," said Kenneth, "a cat can't be queen."

"Sure she can. And I can be a knight in armor."

"No, you can't," said Matt. "You don't have a shield."

"That's because you have our garbage can lid," said Jennifer.

"Well, I'm the king," said Matt. "Look, you can play. But you have to be court wizard and stay at the castle and practice magic."

"What?" said Jennifer. "I don't want to be court wizard. Being court wizard is boring."

"You can be queen or court wizard. And that's final," said Matt.

Matt isn't a good king, Jennifer thought. If I was king, I would let everybody be knights.

But at least Matt hadn't told her she couldn't play at all. She just couldn't be a knight. So Jennifer was the wizard and Guinevere the cat was queen.

King Matt and his knights put on their tunics. They took their swords and shields.

"We shall return in a fortnight," King Matt said. "After we have rid the kingdom of the fire-breathing dragon." Off they went to slay the dragon.

Jennifer took a black cape from her costume box. So what if she couldn't carry a shield? A cape was just as good. She draped it over her shoulders. Almost as good. Then she sat on the back steps with Guinevere. She waited for magic to happen.

Nothing happened.

"I knew this would be boring," Jennifer said to Guinevere.

"Jennifer." Mom came out the back door. "Have you seen Matt?"

"Matt is a king," said Jennifer. "He rode off with his knights to slay a dragon. And he said he'll be back in a fortnight."

"I hope he comes back sooner than that," said Mom.

Jennifer stood up and flapped her cape. "I am a wizard," she said. Then she let her cape droop. "But I really want to be a knight."

"I see," said Mom. "There is a slight problem with being knights, though. T. J.'s mom called. David's dad called. And Kenneth's mom called. They are not happy about their garbage cans. I'm afraid the boys will have to be knights without garbage can lids."

"But they can't," said Jennifer. "Matt said they have to have shields."

"They'll have to come up with something else. I'll talk to Matt when he comes home." Mom went inside.

When the knights came home for a snack, Mom shouted out the door, "Boys, you can't use those garbage can lids. Please put them back where they belong."

"Ah, Mom," King Matt said.

His knights groaned. But they went home to put their shields back on the garbage cans.

"Now what are we supposed to do?" said King Matt. "We can't play knights without shields."

"That's what I told Mom," Jennifer said.

The knights sat around moping in the backyard. Jennifer sat down with them. Moping was even more boring than waiting for magic to happen.

Suddenly Jennifer jumped up. "I've got an idea."

"It won't work," said Matt. "What idea?"

"If you don't think it will work, why
should I tell you?" Jennifer said. "Don't
go away," she told King Matt and his
knights. "I'll be back in a fortnight."

Jennifer and Queen Guinevere went
into the garage. She looked in Dad's
workshop and in the corner she found
a stack of cardboard for recycling.
Jennifer took five big pieces. Next she

got strips of cloth from the ragbag. She stapled the cloth on the back of the cardboard for handles.

Then she got her markers. She started to draw dragons and lions and golden goblets on the cardboard. She wanted to draw everything just right, so she got Matt's book to see exactly what the creatures looked like. She drew a

crown on a lion for Matt because he was king, and she drew a unicorn and a rainbow because she liked unicorns and rainbows.

Finally she finished. She wrapped her cloak around the cardboard. Very quietly she went back outside.

The knights had taken off their tunics. They were running through the castle sprinklers.

"Hear ye! Hear ye!" Jennifer shouted.

"What's up?" said King Matt. He and his knights walked over to see what Jennifer was doing.

She waited until they all stood around her. "*Allie kazoom*," she said, pulling the cape away. "Shields for every knight."

"Gadzooks," said King Matt. "You

are a wizard."

"Now we can play knights again," Sir T. J. said.

"These shields are even better," said Sir Kenneth. "They all have different designs."

Jennifer gave everyone a shield.

"Hey, there's one shield left," said King Matt.

"I know," said Jennifer. "I can count." She held up the shield with the unicorn and rainbow on it. "This one's for me."

King Matt looked very serious.

Uh-oh, thought Jennifer. He's thinking again. He's going to come up with a reason why I can't be a knight.

But then he held up his sword and turned to Jennifer. "I dub you Sir

Jennifer," said King Matt.

Jennifer grinned. She felt like jumping up and down and shouting yippee! Instead she rode off to chase dragons with King Matt and his knights. Many dragons were slain on that day, and the knights had to rescue Queen Guinevere after she got stuck on a tree branch.

"You have proven yourself well," King Matt said to Sir Jennifer, and the other knights agreed.

Jennifer hoped they would play knights in armor tomorrow. She liked playing spies in disguise and telling ghost stories in the attic, but best of all she liked being Sir Jennifer.